Please help the bunnies of Moonglow

Our brave and loyal friend Arrow has come from our world to protect the magical sky. Keep the kingdom safe from the dark rabbits. Arrow is very far from home and will need your help.

Could you be his friend?

This magic bunny might be hard to spot as he is very small and often appears in different fluffy bunny disguises – but you can recognize him by the rainbow twinkle in his eyes.

Thank you for your help!

Strike
Leader of Moonglow Meadow

Sue Bentley's books for children often include animals, fairies and magic. She lives in Northampton in a house surrounded by a hedge so she can pretend she's in the middle of the countryside. She loves reading and going to the cinema, and writes while watching the birds on the feeders outside her window and eating chocolate. Sue was brought up surrounded by small animals and loved them all — especially her gentle pet rabbits whose fur smelled so sweetly of rain and grass.

Sue Bentley

Dancing Days

Illustrated by Angela Swan

PUFFIN

To Nirvana – so sweet. Baby you're the best.

PUFFIN BOOKS

Published by the Penguin Group
Penguin Books Ltd, 80 Strand, London WC2R 0RL, England
Penguin Group (USA) Inc., 375 Hudson Street, New York, New York 10014, USA
Penguin Group (Canada), 90 Eglinton Avenue East, Suite 700, Toronto, Ontario, Canada M4P 2Y3
(a division of Pearson Penguin Canada Inc.)
Penguin Ireland, 25 St Stephen's Green, Dublin 2, Ireland (a division of Penguin Books Ltd)
Penguin Group (Australia), 250 Camberwell Road, Camberwell, Victoria 3124, Australia
(a division of Pearson Australia Group Pty Ltd)
Penguin Books India Pvt Ltd, 11 Community Centre, Panchsheel Park, New Delhi – 110 017, India
Penguin Group (NZ), 67 Apollo Drive, Rosedale, North Shore 0632, New Zealand
(a division of Pearson New Zealand Ltd)
Penguin Books (South Africa) (Pty) Ltd, 24 Sturdee Avenue, Rosebank,
Johannesburg 2196, South Africa

Penguin Books Ltd, Registered Offices: 80 Strand, London WC2R 0RL, England

puffinbooks.com

First published 2010
1

Text copyright © Sue Bentley, 2010
Illustrations copyright © Angela Swan, 2010
All rights reserved

The moral right of the author and illustrator has been asserted

Set in Bembo
Made and printed in England by Clays Ltd, St Ives plc

British Library Cataloguing in Publication Data
A CIP catalogue record for this book is available from the British Library

ISBN: 978–0–141–33243–7

www.greenpenguin.co.uk

Prologue

Arrow jumped into the air and happily kicked out his back legs as he looked round at Moonglow Meadow. His silky white fur, flecked with silver, gleamed in the moonlight. Tiny rainbows shone in his warm brown eyes. It felt good to be back.

His fellow magic rabbits were nibbling juicy leaves or gathering around crystal pools to drink. The moon seemed to turn all the brightly coloured wild flowers into pale jewels.

The grass smelled delicious and Arrow began to eat. The tiny key he wore on a fine chain round his neck tinkled faintly.

Arrow saw a movement from the corner of his eye. An older rabbit with a wise expression and a dark grey muzzle was bounding towards him.

'Strike!' Arrow stopped eating and bowed his head in greeting before the leader of the warren.

'It is good to see you,' Strike said warmly. 'Moonglow Meadow is lush and green again because of the key's magic.'

As chosen keeper of the magical key, it was Arrow's job to look after it. 'I came at once when the key glowed brightly, telling me that more of its magic was needed.'

'We are all thankful to you.' Strike reached out a paw and touched Arrow's shoulder. 'But I have bad news. The dark rabbits are approaching to try to steal the key.'

The dark rabbits lived in a deep gulley next to Moonglow Meadow. Their land had become so dry that nothing grew there any more and they were hungry.

'So they are still unwilling to share our land?' Arrow guessed.

Strike nodded. 'They want to use the key's power to make only *their* gully green and beautiful again.'

'But then *our* meadow would become a desert!' Arrow said, shocked. 'What can we do?'

'You must be brave, Arrow, and go back

to the Otherworld to keep the key safe,'
Strike said.

Arrow felt very young and afraid as he
thought of all the unknown dangers. But
he took a deep breath and nodded slowly.
'I will go.'

Strike smiled with pride and affection.
'Well said.' Then, lifting his head, he gave
a soft but piercing cry.

All the rabbits in the warren pricked
up their ears and came rushing towards
them. They formed a circle round Arrow.
The golden key glowed as brightly as
the sun.

The light slowly faded and where
the young pure-white-and-silver
rabbit had been, there now sat a tiny
fluffy black-and-white bunny with huge
chocolate-brown eyes that gleamed with

tiny rainbows.

'This disguise will protect you. Only return when we need more of the key's magic,' Strike instructed. 'And watch out for dark rabbits!'

Arrow drew himself up. 'I will not fail the warren!'

Thud. Thud. Thud. The rabbits began thumping their feet in time. Arrow felt the magic building and a cloud of crystal dust shimmered around him and Moonglow Meadow began to fade . . .

Chapter
ONE

Sara Penfold bit back tears as she hobbled
across the hospital car park.

'Lean on me. That's it.' Sara's dad
steadied her so she could scoot awkwardly
into the back seat of their car. 'OK?'
he asked. 'At least you'll be able to get
around on those crutches the hospital
has loaned you. And the doctor says your
ankle will soon be as good as new. Things

could be a lot worse.'

'No, they couldn't,' Sara said glumly.
She flicked back her shoulder-length

brown hair as she arranged her long legs across the seat. 'The auditions are next week. Why did this have to happen to me?'

Jane Lewis, her dance teacher, was going to choose four of her best students to form a troupe that would train together every week, and eventually dance at local events.

'Accidents happen sometimes, I'm afraid.' Sara's mum got into the driver's side. She glanced into the rear-view mirror and gave her daughter a sympathetic smile. 'Cheer up, love. There'll be lots of other opportunities.'

Not like this, Sara thought glumly.

She really wanted to develop her dancing skills and become a more confident performer. Being part of a regular troupe would have been perfect for her.

Sara stared fixedly out of the side window at the familiar streets as her mum drove them home, but in her mind she was back at the studio with all her dance friends. Just a couple of hours ago she was enjoying the wonderful feeling of her body moving in time to the music as she learned some new steps.

Then it had happened. She'd landed awkwardly, slipped on to the side of her foot and felt a sharp pain zing through her ankle. The doctor had told her she'd sprained it, and even though it didn't hurt that much now that it was all bandaged up, she'd been told that if she wanted it to heal properly she had to rest it completely.

So no dancing for three whole weeks!

Despite Sara's efforts to put on a brave face, her eyes pricked with tears.

'I wonder what Beth's going to do now?' her dad remarked. 'You two practically live at that studio.'

'I know. I feel really bad for her,' Sara said miserably.

She and Beth were best friends as well as dance partners. They'd been practising a brilliant new routine, ready for Jane's auditions. Now Beth would have to perform it on her own.

Sara remembered something. 'I've left some of my stuff in the lockers at the studio. Could we go and get it, please?'

'Are you sure you want to? I can get it for you any time,' her mum offered.

Sara shook her head. 'Dance classes will have finished for the day, so I can just go in quickly without everyone making a fuss. Anyway, I might as well start getting used to these things.' She waved one of the crutches.

Her mum nodded. 'OK.'

A few minutes later they parked outside the community college. It was an impressive dome-shaped building, always flooded with light from the glass panels that formed its walls. Its wide staircase and high ceiling could be seen through the entrance windows.

Sara's dad helped her out of the car. He walked with her through the automatic front doors and then up to the first floor in the lift. Adults and kids wearing sports kit passed them in the corridor. The smell of freshly brewed coffee met them as they approached the large open-plan cafe.

'I'll be fine now, Dad. The studio's just over there. Why don't you wait here for me?'

'If you're sure,' he said, taking a seat in the cafe. 'Take care on those crutches then.'

'I will.' Sara negotiated the door into the changing rooms next to the studio. She managed to get across the room, but it was difficult to fish her locker key out of her jeans pocket while balancing on crutches.

She carefully propped one of them against the lockers, so she had a hand free. Opening her locker, she reached for a book, a CD and some practice clothes and began stuffing them into a spare holdall that she found crumpled at the back. It was a bit awkward with one hand, but she finally managed it.

As she closed the locker, she didn't
notice that she'd brushed against the
crutch that was propped next to her. It
slid sideways and crashed to the ground.
The loud noise made Sara almost jump
out of her skin and she dropped the
holdall in surprise.

'Oh great! Now what do I do?' she groaned.

There was no point in calling for her dad as he wouldn't hear her through two doors. She'd have to try to bend down to pick up the crutch herself.

'Right. How hard can this be?'

Sara gritted her teeth. Keeping her injured ankle in the air, she balanced on one crutch and tried to crouch down. But then she lost her balance and felt herself falling.

'Oh!' she gasped as she braced herself for a painful landing.

Suddenly, there was a bright flash and a cloud of crystal dust appeared and swirled around Sara. She felt a strange warm tingling sensation down her spine, but the hard bump she expected never came.

To her complete amazement, Sara found herself hovering in mid-air a few centimetres above the floor. She caught her breath as she felt herself turning and then floating gently downwards until she ended up sitting on the floor with her long legs outstretched.

'What just happened?' She felt like pinching herself to see if she was dreaming.

'I hope you are not hurt?' asked a little voice from across the changing room.

Chapter
TWO

Sara looked around and saw a tiny fluffy
black-and-white bunny crouching on
top of the nearest bench. It had big
chocolate-brown eyes and they seemed
to be twinkling with tiny rainbows.
Sara's eyes widened as she tried to make
sense of what had just happened. She
must be more shaken up by her fall
than she thought. She was imagining

the oddest things!

Sara watched as the cute bunny hopped closer towards her – it was definitely real. But there was no way it could have spoken to her!

'How did you get in here?' she thought aloud. 'I wonder if you belong to someone from the dance class?'

'I do not belong to anyone,' the bunny told her. 'I had just arrived here when I saw you fall, so I used my magic to stop you hurting yourself. I am sorry if I startled you.'

Sara did a double take. 'You . . . you really can talk!' she blurted out.

The bunny blinked at her. Despite its tiny size it didn't seem to be afraid of her.

Sara noticed that it wore a tiny gold key on a chain round its neck.

'All the rabbits in my warren can talk. I am Arrow, guardian of Moonglow Meadow and keeper of the key that keeps our meadow lush and green,' the bunny said, lifting his fluffy little head proudly. 'May I know your name?'

'S–Sara. Sara Penfold. I just . . . um . . . called in here to . . . erm . . . pick up some of my stuff,' she stammered. Her mind was still whirling. She couldn't believe this was happening, but she didn't want to scare this amazing bunny away. 'Thanks for saving me from hurting myself.

I could have made my bad ankle even worse.'

'You are welcome!' Arrow bowed his head. 'I am honoured to meet you, Sara.'

'Um . . . me too.' She dipped her head, feeling a bit strange at being so formal while still sitting on the floor with only one trainer on and a heavily bandaged ankle.

Arrow twitched his long floppy ears and his face took on a serious look. 'I need somewhere to hide, and quickly.'

'Why do you need to do that?' Sara asked. 'Is someone after you?'

The black-and-white bunny's brown eyes flashed with sadness and anger.

'Yes. I am in hiding from our neighbours, who are fierce dark rabbits. Their land is dry and stony, but they refuse to share our meadow with us. They want to steal the key and use it to make their own land green again. If they do this, Moonglow Meadow will become a desert.'

'Oh no! That would be terrible!' Sara exclaimed.

'Yes, it would. That is why Strike, our leader, sent me here to keep the magic key safe.'

Sara frowned, puzzled. 'Is Moonglow Meadow near here then – behind the community college?'

The tiny bunny shook his head. 'It is far away. In another world.'

Sara felt her curiosity taking over from her shock. Arrow's homeland sounded so strange and wonderful! 'No offence, but you're very tiny for such an important mission,' she said gently.

Rainbows gleamed more brightly in Arrow's dewy brown eyes. 'Please stay there,' he ordered, rising up on to his back legs.

Sara felt another warm prickling sensation down her spine as the key round his neck began flashing and a cloud of shimmering crystal dust appeared. It swirled round Arrow like a miniature whirlwind, and when it cleared, Sara saw that the cute black-and-white bunny had disappeared. In his place stood the most beautiful and impressive rabbit she had ever seen. It was the size of a large cat and had silky pure-white fur, flecked with silver. The tips of its large ears looked as if they'd been dipped in silver glitter and its glowing chocolate-brown eyes flashed

with jewel-bright rainbows.

'Arrow?' Sara gasped in wonderment.

'Yes, it is still me, Sara,' Arrow said in a smooth velvety voice.

Before she had time to get over the shock of seeing Arrow in his true form, there was a final flash of bright light from

the key round his neck and he reappeared
as a tiny fluffy black-and-white bunny.

'Wow! That's a really cool disguise.'

Arrow shook his head. 'The dark
rabbits will see through it if any of them
find me. I must hide now. Can you help
me, please?'

'Yes! You can live with me!' Sara
decided without a second thought. 'We've
got a big garden with lots of grass and
stuff to eat. Just wait until I tell Mum and
Dad about you. And Beth, she's my best
friend. No one's going to believe it!'

'No, I am sorry, Sara. You cannot tell
anyone about me,' Arrow said seriously.
'You must promise me.'

Sara felt disappointed, especially about
not telling her best friend. She and Beth
always told each other everything. But if

24

it would help to keep the magic bunny
safe, then she was prepared to make an
exception.

'OK then. Cross my heart. I'll have to
smuggle you into our house somehow.
I know, you can get into my holdall . . .'

'Sara?' a voice called out. 'Are you all
right? You've been a long time in there.'

Sara froze and then quickly turned
her head to see her dad coming into the
changing room. A horrified look crossed
his face as he saw her sitting on the floor.

'Oh, my goodness! Have you hurt
yourself? I knew I should have come in
with you!'

'I'm fine. Really,' Sara reassured him.
'I landed on my bottom, not my bad
ankle. But then I couldn't reach the
crutches to get up again.'

From the corner of her eye she saw
Arrow leap off the bench, hop towards
the open holdall lying on the floor and
crawl inside it. But for some reason her
dad didn't seem to notice.

'Have you got everything you wanted
from your locker? Then let's get you back
on your feet!' Her dad helped her get up
and balance on her crutches and then he
picked up the holdall with Arrow inside it.

'Thanks, Dad. Let's go. Mum must be wondering where we've got to,' Sara said as she limped towards the door. All she wanted to do was get Arrow safely back home and then settle in with her secret bunny friend.

Chapter
THREE

When they got home Sara struggled up
to her room, closed the door and put her
holdall on the bed. Arrow immediately
jumped out and sat on the duvet.

He looked round her room with
bright, intelligent eyes.

Sara sat next to him. 'How come
Dad didn't see you get into my bag?'
she asked, stroking the bunny's fluffy

black-and-white fur.

'I used my magic so that only you will
be able to see and hear me,' Arrow told
her, his whiskers twitching.

'You can make yourself invisible? Cool!
That's going to make it much easier for
me to take you out with me.'

Arrow nodded. 'This is a safe place.
I think I will be happy here,' he said. He
yawned sleepily and rubbed his eyes with
one fluffy paw.

Sara smiled at him fondly. It must have
been a long journey for the tiny bunny.
She began tucking the duvet round him
like a cosy nest.

'There you are. Now you can have
a nap.' She kissed the top of his head,
breathing in the sweet smell of his
warm fur.

'Thank you, Sara.' Arrow tucked his nose between his front paws. Almost immediately his breathing changed and snuffly bunny snores rose from his little body.

Just then the phone rang in the hall downstairs. Sara heard her mum answer it and footsteps sounded on the stairs. Her mum poked her head round the door to hand Sara the phone.

'It's Beth for you, love.'

'Thanks, Mum.' Sara took the phone from her eagerly, pleased that her best friend had called. 'Hi, Beth.'

'Sara! How's your ankle? I was so worried about you. Everyone in dance class wants to know if you're OK. Your mum told me you've just got back from hospital. Have you got a plaster cast?'

'No. Just a bandage. My ankle's badly sprained.'

Beth gave a sigh of relief. 'That's not so bad then. You'll have to miss a couple of classes, but we can do extra practice at my house to make up for it. We're totally going to win a place in Jane's new troupe!' she said confidently.

Despite herself Sara grinned. Beth's confidence was one of the things she liked best about her.

'Sorry, Beth, but I won't be able to dance for at least three weeks. That's how long it's going to take for my ankle to heal. I won't be able to make the auditions,' she said quietly.

'Oh no!' Beth exclaimed. 'That's a real pain. I'd *really* set my heart on joining Jane's troupe.'

'Tell me about it,' Sara said glumly, her spirits sinking. 'I've messed things up for both of us, haven't I?'

Finding Arrow had taken her mind off her injury for a little while. But now she realized again how much it affected their dance dreams, both hers *and* Beth's.

'You can't help it. It's just bad luck,' Beth said generously. 'Hang on, Mum's calling me. I'm going to visit my gran for the weekend.' She covered the phone with her hand and yelled, 'Just coming!' then spoke to Sara again. 'You'll be at

school on Monday though, right? I'll see
you then!'

'Yep. Have a good time at your gran's.
Bye, Beth.' Sara put the phone down on
her bedside table.

She sighed. She'd expected Beth
to come round so they could at least
talk and maybe look at some dancing

magazines together. It was going to be
a long weekend without her best friend
around to cheer her up.

Sara looked down at the tiny fluffy
black-and-white bunny. Arrow's little
sides were moving up and down and
his whiskers were twitching as if he was
dreaming. He was so cute, and so brave
to have come here all by himself.

Maybe they could help each other to
feel less lonely.

'I love having you living with me!' Sara
said to Arrow on Monday morning. Even
normal things like having breakfast, doing
homework in her bedroom and watching
TV were fun when you had a magical
friend for company. She'd spent quite
a bit of time with him in the garden,

throwing small twigs for him to bring
back to her or cuddling him while
she read.

Arrow's ears twitched. 'I like it here
with you too.'

'Ready to get inside?' Sara smiled
at him as she finished packing her
school bag.

Arrow nodded and jumped straight in.

Sara's mum gave them a lift to school.
Beth came dashing up the road just as
Sara reached the school gate. 'Hi, Sara!'
she puffed.

'Hi, Beth.' Sara smiled happily as her
friend ran up. She was a bit puzzled about
why she was so out of breath. Beth was
usually there first and waiting to meet her.

She'd been a bit worried that Beth
would be annoyed with her for not

being able to dance their routine for the
audition. But Beth seemed her usual self
as she chatted on their way to class about
her weekend with her grandma.

'So, what did you do?' Beth asked
finally.

'Oh, not much really,' Sara said vaguely.

Beth wouldn't have believed her even
if she could have told her about the

invisible fluffy bunny that was leaning up and looking out of her shoulder bag.

When the bell went, they walked into class together.

The first lesson was maths, which wasn't Sara's favourite subject. She chewed the end of her pen and looked up from her workbook to see what Arrow was doing. His little black-and-white form appeared for a moment between two desks, before he disappeared under them again.

Sara smiled to herself, imagining his little pink nose snuffling up all the interesting smells. After a few minutes, he reappeared from beneath the desk and she saw him making for the nature table.

Arrow reared up on to his back legs to investigate a branch drooping over the side. He nibbled a bit of leaf and seemed to like the taste. His fluffy tail twitched eagerly as he took a firmer grip and started to pull.

'Uh-oh!' Sara breathed.

Birds' nests, leaves and dried plants in empty jam jars that were entangled with the branch began to slide towards the edge of the table. The whole lot was going to tumble on to the tiny bunny at any moment, but Sara was too far away to warn Arrow.

What was she going to do?

Chapter
FOUR

'*Ah-cho-oo-oo!*' Sara sneezed as noisily as possible. '*Hrr-up! Splurgh!*' she coughed.

Beside her, Beth dropped her pencil in surprise.

The teacher frowned and gave Sara a disapproving look. 'Whatever's wrong, Sara? Do you need a glass of water?'

'Sorry, Miss!' Sara apologized. 'I almost ... um ... swallowed a fly! I'm fine now.'

Her classmates giggled, especially Beth.

But it had done the trick. Across the classroom, the noise had made Arrow jump backwards from the table in fright. His magic key glowed brightly and he landed on Sara's desk in a *whoosh* of

crystal dust. His fur was all on end and his body looked as round as a soft fuzzy ball.

'Are you OK?' Sara whispered to him, as everyone went back to work.

'I am fine now,' Arrow told her, shaking himself so his black-and-white fur settled back down. 'What happened?'

'You were about to pull all that stuff on top of you. I had to do something,' she explained. 'It's probably best if you don't nibble things in class. You could get into all sorts of trouble. We'll be going outside at lunchtime, so you can eat some grass.'

'I did wrong. I am a bad bunny.' Arrow buried his face in his front paws.

Sara's heart melted and she only just managed to stop herself picking him up and giving him a cuddle. 'No, you're not! You're my brave little friend,' she whispered.

'Thank you, Sara.' Arrow hunched down next to her pencil case.

'When's it lunchtime? I'm starving!' Beth whispered loudly a few minutes later. She sat back and stretched her arms. 'Must be all the extra practice we did . . . I mean . . . *I* did this morning. Oh, sorry . . .' she trailed off, raising her eyebrows apologetically. 'I don't suppose you want to hear about that.'

'It's OK,' Sara told her with a grin. 'I know I can't dance, but I'm not going to get upset if we talk about it. We did come up with a great routine, didn't we? It's such a shame we won't be performing it for Jane's audition.'

'Um . . . yeah,' Beth said, going red. Ducking her head, she fiddled about in her fake-fur pencil case.

Sara frowned, puzzled. Beth was acting strangely.

Just then, the lunch bell went. Chairs scraped on the floor and desk drawers banged as everyone began filing out of the classroom. 'It's probably best if you get into my shoulder bag,' Sara whispered to Arrow.

'Very well.' With a whisk of his tail, he jumped straight in.

Beth reached behind the desk for Sara's crutches. 'Here you go.'

'Thanks.' Sara stood up and adjusted her weight on the crutches. She had slipped the long strap of her bag over one shoulder, so it hung across her body. That way she could be sure Arrow wasn't jostled about too much as she limped along.

Sara and Beth found a spare bench outside and opened their lunchboxes. Arrow hopped out of the bag and streaked across the grass.

Beth handed Sara an iced cake in a frilly paper case. It had a lemon jelly slice on top. 'Mum made cupcakes. I brought you one.'

'Thanks! Looks yummy!' Beth's mum was a great cook.

When they'd finished eating, they
watched some girls practising dance
moves. Sara knew most of them from her
dance class. One of them, a tall blonde-
haired girl called Olya, was a really good
dancer.

'Hiya!' Olya called, smiling and waving
as she saw Sara watching.

Sara waved back. She turned to say
something to Beth and saw her smiling
widely and giving the blonde girl a
double thumbs up. It looked as if Olya
had been waving at Beth and not her.

Sara was puzzled. What was going on?
She didn't think Beth and Olya were all
that friendly.

Beth turned to watch some girls who
were doing complicated locks and pops.
Sara saw Beth nodding her head in time

to the imaginary music and doing some of the arm movements in time with the other girls. Olya beckoned to her to join them.

Beth jumped to her feet eagerly and looked at Sara. 'Do you mind?'

'Course not. You go on,' Sara said.

She watched them wistfully, hating just having to sit there. Beth, Olya and the girls were having so much fun doing more and more complicated moves.

Sighing, she hoped it wouldn't be too long before her ankle healed and she could dance again.

Arrow had finished eating grass. He hopped back across the playing field towards the bench where Sara sat and stopped beside it to groom himself.

Beth was fooling about, doing a moonwalk as the others clapped. She glided smoothly across the grass as if she was sliding on ice.

Sara tensed. Beth was moving closer to where Arrow sat. He was so busy licking his pale tummy that he hadn't noticed the danger. Any second now, Beth was going to step on her invisible little friend!

'Look out!' she cried, lifting one crutch. She only meant to wave it warningly, but before she could swing it out of the way,

Beth tripped over it.

'Ow!' Beth sprawled full length on
the grass.

Startled, Arrow leapt in the air and
quickly hopped under the bench out
of harm's way.

Beth scrambled to her feet. She
brushed grass off her uniform. 'What
did you do that for, you muppet?' she
shouted.

'I thought you were going to hurt Arr—
I mean bash into my ankle,' Sara quickly
corrected, horrified that she'd almost
given away Arrow's secret. She would
have to be more careful.

'I saw what happened. You tripped
Beth up on purpose,' Olya cried. 'You're
jealous because Beth's asked me to be her
new dance partner!'

Sara looked up in total disbelief as the
tall girl strode towards her, her blonde
hair swinging out behind her.

Chapter
FIVE

Sara gaped at her best friend. 'Beth?
What's Olya talking about? I'm your
dance partner!'

'I was going to tell you,' Beth said,
looking sheepish. 'I just really wanted to
audition for the dance troupe, but our
routine doesn't work as a solo. So I . . .
I asked Olya to dance it with me instead.
That's OK, isn't it?' she said quietly. 'It's

only while your ankle's getting better.
You're still my usual dance partner.'

Sara knew how much winning a place
in Jane's new troupe meant to Beth. But
she had assumed that Beth wouldn't go
in for it without her. What would happen
if Beth got a place and she didn't? She
swallowed hard, trying not to feel upset.

'All right,' she said, nodding slowly.

'Thanks, Sara!' Beth sounded relieved.
'I've been putting off telling you, cos I
was worried that you'd be angry with me.'

'No way! We've been friends forever.'
Sara managed a smile, despite the sinking
feeling in her tummy at being left out. If
Beth and Olya joined Jane's new troupe,
they'd be practising hard and taking extra
classes, but she wouldn't be included.
Would Beth still be her best friend?

'It's a great routine,' Olya said. 'You and Beth must have worked really hard on it. I'm going to dance it the best I can. And I'm sorry for what I said about you tripping Beth up and stuff.'

Sara shrugged. 'That's OK.' Olya actually seemed quite nice. Another time she would have enjoyed dancing with her and Beth. She just hoped that Beth wouldn't like Olya so much that she

decided to become best friends with her instead. Maybe when her ankle was better they could all team up.

The bell went again and everyone began crowding back into school. Sara's spirits sank a bit as she thought of having to sit around while Beth and Olya had all the fun.

Arrow hopped up to Sara's shoulder bag and leapt inside. His big brown eyes shone with affection. 'Thank you for stopping Beth from treading on me.'

'I'd say we're even!' she whispered back. '*You* saved *me* from hurting myself when I fell over in the changing room.'

Arrow nodded, his little nose twitching. 'It is good that friends can help each other.'

Sara smiled at him as she shouldered

her bag and felt herself starting to cheer up a little. The magic bunny was her very own special secret – she would never share him with anyone.

Two days later, Sara and Arrow were sitting in an empty classroom. It was a cool, rather windy day. From outside came the sounds of voices and laughter from the tennis courts and playing fields.

Sara sighed glumly. The teacher had suggested she stay inside to keep warm, so she was catching up on some reading for their class project. But she just couldn't get interested in reading about Vikings today.

'I'm fed up with limping about on these dumb crutches. I can't do anything exciting,' she grumbled, closing the book with a thud.

Sara tried to make a big effort to cheer herself up for Arrow's sake. He didn't deserve such a grumpy friend. She fished a scrap of paper out of her pencil case, scrunched it up and then flicked it across her desk.

Arrow's eyes gleamed brightly. One tiny fluffy front paw shot out and he trapped the paper beneath it.

'Wow! Great reflexes!' Sara was impressed. 'Let's test them some more.'

Arrow looked up at her in puzzlement. 'How are we going to do that?'

'I've got an idea.' Sara collected a few books and then stacked them at intervals on the nearby work surface. She propped others up to make a tunnel. 'There you go. A bunny obstacle course!'

Arrow's whiskers twitched eagerly as he hopped to one end of the course.

'Go, Arrow! Go, Arrow!' Sara encouraged in a singsong voice. 'Go, Arrow!'

Flattening his ears, the magic bunny hopped forward. He jumped over the obstacles and ducked through the tunnel, his bobtail flicking delightedly.

Sara hobbled to one end of the work surface. Propping her crutches against a nearby desk, she opened her arms as Arrow hopped over the last pile of books. He gave a mighty leap and launched himself straight at her.

Sara caught him and gave him a big hug. She kissed the top of his fluffy head. 'Yay! This beats playing outside. You'd definitely get a place in the bunny Olympics!'

'It was good fun!' Arrow agreed, gently touching her chin with his pink nose.

'Come on. Let's go for a walk to the cloakrooms and back. Most kids are outside, so you can hop about for a change without worrying about being stepped on.'

She picked up her crutches and they set off down the corridor. As they reached another empty classroom, Sara thought she saw something moving. The door was partly open, so she stopped to look.

There was a girl dancing in the centre of the room. She was slim with striking dark red hair and pale skin and looked about ten years old – a year or so older than her. Sara couldn't remember ever seeing the girl in the playground.

'I wonder who she is,' she whispered to Arrow.

They stood in the doorway silently watching as the girl danced around the room. She was doing a series of complicated spins, twists and locks.

'Wow! She's *really* good!' Sara whispered, totally spellbound as the girl finished her routine with a graceful downward sweep of one arm. She couldn't contain herself any longer. Pushing the door wide open, she went in. 'That was amazing! Where did you learn to dance like that?' she exclaimed.

The girl whipped round, a look of

shock on her face. 'Oh! I . . . I didn't
know anyone was there!' she said,
flustered. 'I didn't mean to . . . Sorry, I've
. . . um . . . gotta go!' As she grabbed her
bag from a nearby desk, something fell
to the floor. But in her haste, the girl
didn't notice.

'Hey, wait!' Sara started forward as the
girl dashed away towards a door in the far
corner of the room. 'What's your name?'

There was no answer. The girl had gone.

Arrow hopped into the room and went

over to the crumpled object on the floor.
Grasping it in his teeth, he dragged it over
to Sara.

'Thanks, Arrow. Look, it's a gym shirt.'
She read the name tag. 'Tamara Blake. I
wonder why she ran away like that?'

Arrow shook his head. 'I do not know.'

Sara nodded in agreement. 'Strange,
wasn't it? If I could dance like that, I'd
be really proud of myself.' She draped
the gym shirt over a chair before she and
Arrow continued on their walk.

Chapter
SIX

After school finished for the day, Sara and
Arrow waited for Beth by the main gate.
'Beth's coming home with us tonight.
Mum's treating us to a pizza,' Sara told
Arrow.

'What is pizza?' Arrow's whiskers
twitched in curiosity.

'It's sort of flat bread with tomatoes
and other stuff, topped with melted

cheese. Wait until you taste it. You'll love it!' She decided to ask for one with lots of spinach, especially for Arrow.

Arrow licked his lips. 'I like trying new human food.'

Sara smiled as she stroked his soft little front paws that were poking out from her shoulder bag. 'I can't decide whether to

tell Beth about Tamara,' she mused, changing the subject.

Arrow looked up at her, a tiny rainbow gleaming in each big brown eye. 'Tamara might not want anyone to know she was dancing by herself.'

Sara thought Arrow could be right. She didn't even know the red-haired girl, but there was something about her she liked and she didn't feel right about snitching on her.

She chewed at her lip. 'I know,' she agreed, 'but Beth's my best friend. We usually tell each other everything. It feels strange to keep secrets from her.'

Arrow lifted a paw and placed it on her hand. 'It is not your secret. It is Tamara's,' he said quietly.

Sara smiled at her wise friend. 'You're

right! Let's keep this just between you
and me for now.'

'Sara!' Beth came out of school. She
waved and quickened her steps as she
hurried towards Sara and Arrow. 'I hope
you weren't too bored all by yourself
while we were playing tennis.'

'Oh, I found loads to do,' Sara said
vaguely. *Like having fun with my magic
bunny friend and finding a mystery dancer!*
'Mum's over there. Let's go!'

'Um . . . sorry, Sara,' Beth said,
wrinkling her nose in apology. 'But I can't
come for a pizza after all. I've got to meet
Olya. We're doing extra practice in the
evenings all week.'

'What, *every* evening?' Sara said,
surprised. 'And sometimes before
school too?'

'Yes, Olya wants to be the best she can for Jane's auditions,' Beth said reasonably.

Sara nodded, not very happy about it. Beth was her best friend after all, and she wasn't used to having to share her. 'I suppose I'd want to do extra practice if it was me,' she said reluctantly. 'Well – see you tomorrow at school.'

'Sure. Bye!' Beth said, walking away.

Sara waved, knowing that Beth's mind was already on her dancing.

Sighing, she felt her thoughts turning to Tamara. How odd that Beth and Olya were rehearsing so much and yet someone as talented as Tamara Blake chose to hide away and dance by herself in an empty classroom.

It didn't make sense.

'Mm–mm. Mushrooms, olives and extra spinach with a cheesy stuffed crust. This is the best!' Sara and Arrow sat in the garden. She helped herself to another slice from the open box.

Beth might not be here, but it was fun to share with Arrow and especially watch him enjoying his very first taste of pizza.

Sara folded a long string of mozzarella into her mouth. 'I've got a new DVD of Shanilla Jakes. She's one of my favourite performers. We could watch it together,' she suggested.

Arrow nodded, still munching. 'I would like that.'

'Come on then. I'll ask to borrow

Mum's laptop. You and I can cuddle up together on my bed and watch it!'

Her mum carried the laptop upstairs for her. Arrow stretched out full length beside her on the bed. Sara loaded the DVD and the screen filled with colourful images.

Arrow's little face lit up in wonder. 'How is this world trapped in a box?' he asked, his whiskers tickling her fingers.

It was a difficult question and Sara tried to explain.

'Well – those moving pictures were filmed from real life. But what we're watching is like a memory – kind of. I don't really know how DVDs work,' she admitted with a grin. 'I just enjoy watching them. Wow! Look at the way Shanilla Jakes moves! Isn't she great?

I wish I could dance like that.'

Arrow looked up at her with rainbow-
bright brown eyes. 'I am sure you will be
a very good dancer one day.'

'Thanks, Arrow,' she said, smiling at
her loyal friend. 'I know it would help
me to get better if I got a place in Jane's
new troupe. Oh well. There's no point
in going on about it.' Sara felt a pang of
sadness as she thought about Beth and
Olya rehearsing together right now.

'Is there not another dance troupe you
could join?' Arrow asked, rubbing his
fluffy cheek against her arm.

Sara stroked his velvety ears. 'I don't
think so. Not round here anyway. I s'pose
someone else might start one up. You
never know,' she said hopefully.

Lights flashed and created dramatic

shadows in the music video playing on the laptop. For a second, the shadows merged together and made a strange rabbit-shaped image on the screen.

Arrow gave a squeal of fright. 'My enemies have found me!' he cried.

'What? Where?' Sara said, puzzled. 'Oh, you mean that rabbit-shaped shadow on the –'

Arrow wasn't listening. Leaping on to the floor, he shot straight towards the open bedroom door. To Sara's horror, he rushed outside and she heard his nails scrabbling on the wooden stairs.

'Oh no!' she gasped. There was no telling where he'd go in his panic.

She clambered down from the bed. Not wanting to waste time reaching for her crutches, she hopped after the terrified bunny on one leg. Holding the stair rail, Sara followed him downstairs as quickly as she could.

The sound of the TV came from the sitting room. Luckily, her parents were watching their favourite television programme.

'Arrow! Stop!' Sara hissed, not daring to raise her voice in case her mum and dad came out to ask what she was doing without her crutches.

Steadying herself on the wall, she went

into the kitchen and glimpsed Arrow's
bobtail through the open back door as
he shot under the patio table. Sara went
outside and lowered herself awkwardly to
the ground. Arrow was tucked into a tight
ball behind the table leg. She crawled
towards him and gently picked him up.

'It's OK. There are no bad rabbits here,'
she crooned, cuddling him in her arms. 'It
was just a trick of the light. DVDs aren't
real, remember?'

But Arrow was still trembling and
didn't seem to have heard her.

Sara felt a tingling sensation down
her spine as his key flashed and a crystal
cloud appeared. It surrounded her and
Arrow and shimmered as it turned into
something fluffy and squishy that felt like
a huge soft duvet.

'Oh!' To Sara's total amazement, she felt
herself floating upwards with Arrow next
to her. They were hovering high in the air
on a soft sparkling white cloud, out of
sight of anyone below! The old apple tree
in the garden was far below them and the
neighbouring gardens were spread out
like brightly coloured patchwork.

Sara glanced at Arrow, who crouched next to her, peeping over the pillowy edge. His whiskers twitched nervously as he searched for signs of his enemies.

'See? There are no dark rabbits anywhere, or you'd be able to see them from way up here,' she reassured him gently. 'Now do you believe me?'

He nodded slowly. 'You are right, Sara. I am sorry I panicked.' His long floppy ears drooped. 'I must try to be brave.'

'You are brave,' Sara said gently. 'And you can do the most amazing things too! I can't believe we're up here – I've never thought that our house and garden could look so beautiful!'

As she looked at him the key round his neck began flashing more brightly than she'd ever seen it.

'Moonglow Meadow will soon be in need of the key's power,' Arrow told her.

Sara's chest tightened with panic. 'Do . . . do you have to leave right now?' she asked worriedly.

'No. Not until the key glows steadily. Then I will know that its magic is needed urgently. If that happens, I will have to leave at once, maybe without saying goodbye.'

Sara knew that she would have to be very strong if that happened, but she couldn't bear to think of it right now. She decided to try to enjoy every moment she could with Arrow.

Just as Sara was wondering where else she and Arrow might be able to go on their magical sparkling cloud, she heard a noise below.

'Sara?' It was her mum's voice coming from the house as she called upstairs. 'I'm going to make a cool drink. I'll bring you one up!'

Chapter
SEVEN

Sara stiffened. 'Oh no! Mum thinks I'm still watching the DVD. She's going to wonder where I am when she goes into my bedroom. What shall I do?'

'Do not worry. We'll float back in through your bedroom window before she notices. But I have used my magic so we have a little time to spare. I thought you might like to enjoy being able to float on this cloud with me for a while.'

'Oh yes. It's so . . . magical. Better than anything!'

'Better than dancing?' Arrow asked cheekily.

She grinned. 'Nothing's better than dancing. But this is close!'

Sara looked around. From high up above the tree, she could see across all the back gardens down the street.

Two gardens away, she spotted a small figure on a lawn. It was a girl with dark-red hair and she was dancing.

Sara narrowed her eyes as she felt a surge of excitement. 'I think that's Tamara Blake! I wondered why I hadn't seen her around. Her family must have only just moved into that empty house. Let's go closer. Will she be able to see us?'

'No, I used my magic so we are both invisible.'

Arrow and Sara gently floated towards the garden where Tamara was dancing. Once again, just like in the classroom, Tamara seemed lost in her own private world of dance. She dipped and spun and struck graceful poses.

A younger girl, who looked very like Tamara, came out of the house. The moment Tamara glimpsed her sister, she stopped dancing. She quickly grabbed a book that was sitting nearby on a table and pretended to be reading.

Sara frowned, puzzled. 'Tamara really hates anyone seeing her dancing. I wonder if it's because she's shy,' she said thoughtfully. 'Going to dance classes every week helped me feel more confident. Maybe they'd help her too.'

'You could tell her about them,' Arrow suggested.

Sara hadn't thought that far ahead. But maybe Arrow was right.

Arrow's brown eyes suddenly lit up with urgency. 'We must leave! It is time for you to be back in your bedroom.'

Everything seemed to go into fast forward. As the sparkling magical cloud

whooshed downwards, Sara and Arrow
bounced on its billowy surface. They
reached her window in the blink of an
eye. Sara giggled as she felt a ticklish
stretching sensation and they whooshed
in through her open window.

She landed in a heap on her bed
and the sparkling cloud dissolved into
sugary dust around her and disappeared.
Sara dashed a hand through her tousled
hair and quickly sat up just as her mum
walked into the room holding a tray.

'Here you are, love. I've brought you a snack as well.'

'Thanks, Mum.'

Sara glanced at Arrow, who was nestled against her pillow. *That was close*, she thought, biting back a grin. Floating on a cloud with her magic bunny friend was the best fun ever!

Chapter
EIGHT

Saturday morning dawned bright and
clear. Sara woke from a wonderful dream.
She had been dancing in a forest, where
every tree glittered with crystal droplets.

'I love how it feels when I dance. It's
the best!' she said, stretching. 'I've decided
to go and watch Beth and Olya dance
in the audition. It's no good being all
moody, just because I can't audition. And

I know how much this means to Beth.'

Arrow was curled up on the pillow near her shoulder. He opened one sleepy brown eye.

'You are a good friend to Beth. And a kind person, Sara.'

'When I haven't got the grumps, you mean?' She laughed wryly. 'I've been thinking about Tamara too. I'm going to try to find out why she dances in secret.'

'How are you going to do that?' Arrow stretched out his front paws and then his back legs, before giving himself a shake.

Sara drew him gently into her arms and stroked his warm fur. 'I reckon I need some way of getting her to talk to me. I've got an idea! How about if we . . .'

Arrow listened intently as Sara finished explaining. He twitched his ears in agreement. 'That is a good plan.'

'Let's do it!' Sara threw back the duvet
and reached for her clothes.

Straight after breakfast, she told her
mum she was going to the corner shop to
buy some sweets with her pocket money.
It wasn't exactly a fib, as Tamara's house
was on the way.

'This is it,' Sara whispered when they
reached the front gate. 'You know what
to do.'

Arrow's big brown eyes glinted with
tiny rainbows. His magic key glowed
brightly. 'I am no longer invisible.'

'Good. Ready?'

Arrow nodded. Hopping under the
front gate, he hopped up the short path.

Sara waited until her magic bunny
was hidden behind a large plant pot near

the front door. She took a deep breath,
hobbled up to the front door and rang
the doorbell. There was a pause and then
Tamara herself opened the door.

'Yes?' she said, smiling. She was even
prettier close up, with lovely hazel eyes.

'Hi! I'm . . . um . . . Sara Penfold. I live
just down the street. I'm looking for my
pet rabbit. He's escaped. I think he might
be in your front garden.'

'Oh, the poor little thing. He must be really scared. I'll help you look for him.' Tamara stepped outside. 'What does he look like?'

'Thanks.' Sara smiled gratefully. 'He's tiny with fluffy black–and–white fur, a cute pink nose and huge chocolate-brown eyes.'

Arrow saw his chance. He hopped forward and paused for a second on the path to make sure they saw him. He then slipped past Tamara and dashed into a clump of flowers.

'There he is!' Tamara cried, running after him. 'I'll get him!'

Sara grinned to herself. The plan was working!

Arrow flattened his ears and darted about in circles, pretending to be a scared little tame bunny.

Tamara made a grab for him. 'Got you!' she cried triumphantly.

'Phew!' Sara let out a big sigh of relief. 'I didn't think I'd ever catch him.'

'Hello, bunnykins,' Tamara crooned. She held Arrow gently, but firmly. 'Isn't he gorgeous? His eyes are like melted chocolate with rainbow glitter mixed in. How long have you had him?'

'Not very long,' Sara said vaguely. 'But I love him to bits. Thanks very much for helping me to catch him. He's called Arrow.'

'Cool name.' Tamara smiled, as she handed Arrow over. 'Did you say you live just up the road? Do you go to Denton School?'

'Yes. I do. I think I saw you the other

day,' Sara said casually. 'I walked past an empty classroom. And you were dancing –'

'That was you?' Tamara interrupted, blushing.

'Yes. I dance too. Well – I did, before I hurt my ankle. I go to dance classes at the community college with my best friend, Beth,' Sara rushed on quickly, hoping that Tamara would stay and listen to her this time. 'Jane Lewis, the teacher, is really nice. She's starting a new dance troupe. Beth and I were planning to audition together to win a place.'

'That's bad luck,' Tamara said. 'You must be really disappointed.'

'I was for a while,' Sara admitted. 'Beth's still going to dance our routine. She's asked Olya, another girl from our class, to be her partner. The auditions are tomorrow. I'm going to go and cheer them on. Would you like to come with me?'

'Me?' Tamara said, surprised. 'I . . . I don't know.'

'It'll be fun,' Sara encouraged. 'And everyone is really friendly.'

'I really used to love dancing and performing, but I was bullied for showing off at my old school,' Tamara said quietly.

Suddenly everything made sense. Sara felt annoyed on Tamara's behalf.

'I hate kids like that! I bet they were jealous because you're so good. We're not like that here. *I'm* not like that. You'll see. If you come to the auditions, you can meet everyone and then maybe you'd like to come to dance classes with me sometime?'

Tamara seemed to be considering it. 'I've really missed dancing with other people. Maybe it's time I gave it another try. And I'd like to make some new friends round here.' A slow smile spread over her face. 'OK then.'

'Fantastic! My mum's taking me. We'll pick you up at five thirty tomorrow.'

'I'll be ready.'

At the front gate, Sara turned and

waved to Tamara. 'Bye!' She looked at Arrow as they headed home. 'Well done, Arrow. You were great. Our plan worked perfectly.'

'I am glad. I like Tamara.' He nuzzled her hand.

Sara rubbed the soft place between his ears. 'Me too. I hope she'll like Beth and Olya. It would be great to have another dance friend.'

Chapter
NINE

'I hope Tamara hasn't changed her mind about coming with us,' Sara said to Arrow the following day.

But she needn't have worried. Tamara was waiting outside her house when they drew up in her mum's car. Sara grinned.

'Hi!' Tamara greeted Sara warmly. 'Thanks for picking me up, Mrs Penfold.'

'You're welcome,' Sara's mum said, smiling.

'Hi, Tamara,' Sara said as Tamara got into the back and sat next to her and Arrow. 'I phoned Beth to tell her we're coming. She's looking forward to meeting you.'

'Me too,' Tamara said.

The roads were unusually busy and they crawled along, waiting in endless traffic queues. It seemed as if every set of traffic lights was on red. Sara began fidgeting with impatience.

'I wish we could go faster. We're going to be late,' she whispered to Arrow.

'This traffic is bad,' Mrs Penfold said. 'I'm going to try another way.'

They made for the outskirts where the roads were a bit clearer. Sara breathed a sigh of relief. They might still make it if they were lucky. But her mum had just crossed a roundabout when there was a loud clunk! The engine cut out.

'Hold on, girls!' Mrs Penfold cried, pressing a button to switch on the hazard lights. 'I'm going to coast towards that lay-by.' Moments later, they drew to a halt.

'Oh no! Now we'll definitely miss Beth and Olya's dance!' Sara said unhappily.

'At least we're all OK. Your mum was great. She didn't panic or anything,' Tamara said. 'Mine would have had kittens!'

'Yeah, Mum's good at staying calm.' Sara grinned, liking Tamara more and more as she spent more time with her.

Mrs Penfold had spotted a picnic area, set back from the road. 'We'll all go and sit over there and I'll phone for help.'

They got out of the car. Sara began limping over to the wooden tables and benches on her crutches, with Arrow hopping beside her. Tamara was just ahead of them.

Sara felt a familiar warm tingling down her spine and noticed that Arrow's key was flashing and a small cloud of sparkly mist was drifting back towards the car. She turned to watch as it swirled round the bonnet before sinking into it and disappearing.

'You've fixed it for us! Thanks, Arrow. You're a star!' Sara whispered.

'You are welcome,' Arrow said warmly.

'Come on!' Sara called to Tamara, already hobbling back towards her mum, who stood beside the car.

'Where are we going?' Tamara asked.

Sara didn't answer. She reached her mum just as she had got out her phone to call for help. 'Mum! Wait! Try to start the car again first!'

Mrs Penfold blinked at her daughter in disbelief. 'What are you talking about, love? You saw what happened.'

'I know. But I've got this really weird feeling. I *know* it will start. Just try it once more. *Please!*' Sara insisted.

Her mum shook her head slowly. 'All right. But I don't know what good it will do,' she said reluctantly.

She got back in and turned the key in the ignition. *Brrr-rrrrm!* It started like a rocket. 'Would you believe it? It's just like magic!' Mrs Penfold exclaimed in amazement.

Sara smiled, but stayed silent. She, Arrow and Tamara piled back into the car and they were soon on their way. This time there were no hold-ups. They reached the dance studio just as the doors opened and people began filing out.

'The auditions must have finished!' Sara realized with dismay. 'I hope Beth and

Olya haven't left yet. Let's go and see!'

Arrow looked out from her shoulder bag as she went inside with Tamara at her side. She saw Beth and Olya sitting at one side of the studio, opposite the wall of full-length mirrors. Both of them looked downcast.

'What happened?' Sara asked Beth, although she thought she knew.

Beth sighed. 'We didn't get picked,' she said quietly. 'Jane said it was a difficult choice because the standard was really high, but in the end she picked four other girls.'

Olya shrugged. 'There's always next time. It's not the end of the world.'

'Isn't it?' Beth said glumly.

Sara felt a pang of disappointment for Beth. Mixed feelings swept through her. She felt sad for her competitive best friend, whose hopes had been dashed. But also relieved that Beth wasn't going to be spending lots of time training in a new troupe without her.

'I'm sorry, Beth. You and Olya couldn't have worked any harder,' Sara said with feeling. She suddenly realized that Tamara was standing beside her. She was looking at the floor and fiddling with her hands. Maybe it wasn't the best time to introduce her, but they were here now. 'This is Tamara. She's just moved into my street. She's a brilliant dancer and she's thinking about coming to dance classes with us.'

'Hi, Tamara,' Beth said, looking curious despite herself.

'Hi,' Olya said.

'Sara told me about the auditions. I'm sorry you didn't get into the troupe,' Tamara said shyly.

'Thanks,' Beth and Olya said together.

Suddenly, Beth stood up and linked arms with Sara. 'Sorry to be such a grump. I'm sure there'll be other chances. How's your ankle feeling anyway? I've really missed dancing with you.'

'Me too,' Sara said happily, smiling at
her best friend. Her eyes sparkled. 'But I'll
soon be back in my dancing shoes. Then
watch out!'

Beth laughed and Olya and Tamara
joined in.

Tamara's whole face had brightened. 'I've decided – I'm definitely going to come to classes with all of you. It's going to be great to have some new dance fr–'

But Sara didn't hear the rest of what Tamara was saying because Arrow's key suddenly began to glow more brightly than she'd ever seen it. He leapt out of her bag in a whoosh of crystal dust that was twinkling with rainbow sparkles, and tore off down the corridor.

Sara's heart missed a beat. The moment she had been dreading was here!

Without a second thought, she hobbled after him and just caught a glimpse of him darting into a storeroom. She went in to find Arrow sitting there in his true form – a tiny fluffy black-and-white bunny no longer, but a magnificent rabbit the size of a large cat. His silky pure-white fur was flecked with silver and his large ears had glittering silver tips.

'Arrow!' Sara gasped. She'd forgotten that her friend was so majestic. 'You're leaving right now, aren't you?'

Arrow's chocolate-brown eyes softened with sadness. 'Yes. Moonglow Meadow urgently needs more of the key's magic.'

Sara nodded silently, her eyes brimming with tears. She knew she had to be brave and let him go. Arrow hopped over and reared up on to his back legs, so she could reach down to stroke him. Her fingers brushed against his warm silken fur.

'I'll never forget you,' she said, her voice breaking.

'Nor I you. You have been a good friend, Sara.' Arrow let her stroke him

for one final time and then moved away.
'Farewell. Always follow your dreams,' he
said in a soft velvety voice.

There was a final flash of light, and
crystal dust trickled down around Sara
and made a sound like the ringing of
fairy bells as it hit the ground. Arrow
faded and was gone.

Sara stood there, still not quite believing that she'd never see Arrow again. She swallowed her tears with an effort. Something lay on top of a nearby cardboard box. It was a single crystal rainbow drop. She reached out to pick it up. The drop tingled against her fingers as it turned into a tiny pure-white pebble in the shape of a bunny.

Sara slipped it into her pocket. She knew she would keep it forever as a reminder of the magic bunny and their time together. As she went out of the storeroom, Beth ran up to her.

'There you are! Tamara's great, isn't she? In fact, we were just talking and I've had the best idea!'

Sara frowned. How come Beth looked so happy all of a sudden? 'What idea?'

'To form *our own* dance troupe,' Beth enthused. 'The four of us – you, me, Olya and Tamara. It's going to be brilliant!'

Sara felt a smile spreading across her face. She knew that Arrow would be really pleased for her.

Say 'Hi' to the other magic bunnies for me. And look after Moonglow Meadow, she whispered under her breath.

Olya and Tamara came towards them with linked arms. Tamara was beaming with happiness.

'So, what are we going to call our troupe?' asked Olya.

'How about "The Arrows"?' Sara said happily.

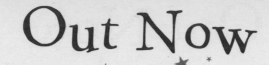

Out Now

Magic Bunny

Could you be this tiny bunny's special friend?

Magic Bunny

Chocolate Wishes

SUE BENTLEY

puffin.co.uk

Out Now

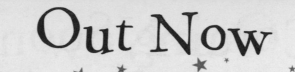

Magic Bunny

Could you be this tiny bunny's special friend?

Magic Bunny

Holiday Dreams

SUE BENTLEY

puffin.co.uk

Coming Soon

Magic Bunny

Could you be this tiny bunny's special friend?

Magic Bunny

Classroom Capers

SUE BENTLEY

Coming Soon

Magic Bunny

Could you be this tiny bunny's special friend?

Magic Bunny
A Splash of Magic

SUE BENTLEY

puffin.co.uk

Magic Ponies

A New Friend
9780141325934

A Special Wish
9780141325941

A Twinkle of Hooves
9780141325958

Showjumping Dreams
9780141325965

Seaside Summer
9780141325972

Riding Rescue
9780141325989

Winter Wonderland
9780141327723

Pony Camp
9780141327730

A Christmas Wish
9780141325996

puffin.co.uk

Magic Puppy

A New Beginning
9780141323503

Muddy Paws
9780141323510

Cloud Capers
9780141323527

Star of the Show
9780141323534

Party Dreams
9780141323794

A Forest Charm
9780141323800

Twirling Tails
9780141323817

School of Mischief
9780141323824

Snowy Wishes
9780141323831

Classroom Princess
9780141324791

Friendship Forever
9780141324784

Sparkling Skates
9780141324777

Sunshine Shimmers
9780141324760

Spellbound at School
9780141324753

The Perfect Secret
9780141324746

A little puppy
a sprinkling of magic,
a forever friend

puffin.co.uk

If you like Magic Puppy, you'll love

Magic Kitten

A Summer Spell
9780141320144

Classroom Chaos
9780141320151

Star Dreams
9780141320168

Double Trouble
9780141320175

Moonlight Mischief
9780141321530

A Circus Wish
9780141321547

Sparkling Steps
9780141321554

A Glittering Gallop
9780141321561

Seaside Mystery
9780141321981

Firelight Friends
9780141321998

A Shimmering Splash
9780141322001

A Puzzle of Paws
9780141322018

A Christmas Surprise
9780141323237

Picture Perfect
9780141323480

A Splash of Forever
9780141323497

Magic Bunny

Win a Magic Bunny goody bag!

Strike, the leader of the bunnies of Moonglow Meadow, has an urgent message for Arrow that will keep him safe from the dark rabbits who are trying to capture the magic key.

Two words from the message can be found in the special carrots that are hidden in *Holiday Dreams* and *Dancing Days*. Find the hidden words and put them together to complete Strike's message. Send it in to us and each month we will put every correct message in a draw and pick out one lucky winner who will receive a special Magic Bunny prize.

Send your secret message, name and address on a postcard to:
Magic Bunny competition
Puffin Books
80 Strand
London WC2R 0RL

Hurry, Arrow needs your help!

Good luck!

puffin.co.uk

It all started with a Scarecrow.

Puffin is seventy years old.
Sounds ancient, doesn't it? But Puffin has never been
so lively. We're always on the lookout for the next big
idea, which is how it began all those years ago.

Penguin Books was a big idea from the mind of
a man called Allen Lane, who in 1935 invented
the quality paperback and changed the world.
**And from great Penguins, great Puffins grew,
changing the face of children's books forever.**

The first four Puffin Picture Books were hatched in 1940 and the
first Puffin story book featured a man with broomstick arms called
Worzel Gummidge. In 1967 Kaye Webb, Puffin Editor, started the
Puffin Club, promising to **'make children into readers'**.
She kept that promise and over 200,000 children became
devoted Puffineers through their quarterly instalments of
Puffin Post, which is now back for a new generation.

Many years from now, we hope you'll look back and
remember Puffin with a smile. **No matter what your age
or what you're into, there's a Puffin for everyone.**
The possibilities are endless, but one thing is for sure:
whether it's a picture book or a paperback, a sticker book
or a hardback, **if it's got that little Puffin
on it – it's bound to be good.**